I0538038

The Rise of

Lucious Morningside

A Kenya Clark Novella

Mahogany SilverRain

This is a work of fiction. Names, characters, places, and incidents either are the product of the author's imagination or are used fictitiously. Any resemblance to actual persons, living or dead, events, or locales is entirely coincidental.

The Rise of Lucious, Book Two, The Kenya Clark Series

Copyright © 2019 Mahogany SilverRain

All rights reserved. Without limiting the rights under copyright reserved above, no part of this publication may be reproduced, stored in or introduced into a retrieval system, or transmitted, in any form, or by any means (electronic, mechanical, photocopying, recording, or otherwise) without the prior written permission of both the copyright owner and the above publisher of this book. This is a work of fiction. Names, characters, places, brands, media, and incidents either are the product of the author's imagination or are fictitious. The author acknowledges that trademarked status and trademark owners of various products may be referenced in this work of fiction. The publication/use of these trademarks is not authorized, associated with, nor sponsored by the trademark owners.

Copyright © 2019 Mahogany SilverRain

Published by Mahogany's Place LLC
ISBN: 978-1-64713-181-4
www.mahoganysilverrain.net

Table of Contents

One

Darrin and Kenya arrived at Empire Park where typically you would find children playing on the playground, people playing tennis or basketball, or walking their dogs along the trails. The only thing Kenya and Darrin saw were police, paramedics, and firefighters. Chaos, smoke and fear filled the air as several people were being treated on the scene, scorched patches of land and a few small fires that firefighters were working to put out. What stood out to Kenya was the two children who stood alone, their backs against a fence, holding on tightly to each other. They were twin girls, eighty years old, both with braided black hair and deep set dark brown eyes filled with terror. Their skin, a smooth deep brown, was flawless. Kenya's heart went out to them. Surrounded by law enforcement, with their guns pointing directly at them, no one was daring to approach to them. Fearing the worst,

Kenya stepped into the fray, "put your weapons down! They're just children!"

"No offense ma'am, but these kids are dangerous! One shoots fire from her hands!" one officer answered. "They are *still* children, and can't you see how scared they are? No, we are NOT killing any kids today!" Kenya shouted. "Let me talk to them, alright?" she pleaded.

One sergeant in charge stepped up to stop her. "Ma'am, I'd advise you not..." he began.

Kenya flashed her federal GBI credentials and her frustration.

The sergeant nodded and stepped back, allowing her to pass. "It's your funeral," he said.

Not today it isn't. She turned to face the girls, a smile on her face to hide her growing fear for *them*. The frightened girls just stared at her, their hearts beating wildly in their chest as a few tears slipped from eyes that began to glow. Kenya put her hands up to show them they did not need to be afraid of her. "I want to help you. I won't hurt you. My name is Kenya Clark. What are your names?" Kenya asked softly.

Her Sig Sauer P228 pistol was firmly in her shoulder

holster on her left, hidden by her heavy blue jacket with GBI spelled out in yellow on the back.

A heavy wind began to blow about them as one girl answered, "I don't want to hurt you either lady, I am Mia, and this is my sister Kia."

"Nice to meet you Mia and Kia. Are you both alright? Are you hurt in any way?" The girls shook their heads. "Good. Can you tell me what happened here?" Kenya asked as she continued to slowly step closer to the girls who began to calm down. As they did, the wind became a light breeze. Kenya turned back to the officers and military personnel, nodding her head and motioning for them to put their guns away. Most did, but a couple were not so easily swayed.

Mia, the more outgoing of the two girls, spoke first as she cautiously eyed the men and women who still had their guns pointed at her. "I don't really know, I was pushing my sister on the swings and then I felt really hot. I hurt my sister's back by accident and then some other kids came over to us when Kia fell off the swing, crying and screaming. The kids came closer and it got really windy. Kia stood up and stopped crying like she didn't hurt anymore. The kids started to tease us and I just put my hand out and...fire, it just came out of my hands!" Mia said as fresh tears began to fall.

Kenya put herself in front of them, blocking the view of the officers behind her.

Kia spoke up, "Mia burned some of them kids and then some big people too. Can you really help us?" Kia's pleading eyes looked up at Kenya.

"I will try sweetheart, I promise. I need you to be calm and keep your hands at your side. Can you do that for me?" Kenya asked sweetly as she knelt down to their level. Both girls nodded. "Good, now where are your parents?" Kenya noticed the eyes of the twins returned to their normal brown color.

"Our Mom died, we never had a dad. We live with a foster family, The McNeals, but they got hurt when Mia..." Kia's voice trailed off as she began to cry in earnest. Mia hugged her and told her everything would be fine. Kenya instinctively reached for them both, holding them to her. She immediately felt their pain, then slowly, their powers. She began to see in her mind exactly what happened on the playground. It was as if she was one of the twins. It was strange, she was not holding an object and yet, she began to see. The powers that the twins held was not truly their own from birth.

She began to hear a voice. "How do you like your new sisters? They are quite special, don't you agree?" Then the voice began to laugh.

Lucious? But how? Why? Before she could get any answers, the vision stopped and she felt both girls go limp in her arms, shot with tranquilizer darts. Kenya turned around to see who shot them as several people in military uniforms approached them, Darrin following close behind. *Dammit!*

"Who gave the order to tranquilize these girls? They're just kids! You can't treat them this way!" Kenya yelled at the two men who not so gently pulled the girls away from her. It reminded Kenya of the horrible teasing she got when she was a kid because of her 'gift' and felt sympathetic toward the twins.

"Where are you taking them?" Kenya demanded. No one answered for a few moments until Kenya yanked on the arm of a military officer. The officer yanked her arm away. "We are taking them to a secure location."

Kenya tried to press for more information, but Darrin pulled her back. "We work for the government, we can get answers, but not this way," he whispered in her ear.

Kenya nodded as tears filled her eyes and threatened to fall. She silently prayed nothing would happen to those beautiful little girls. She would find out where they were going and make them normal again. *Lucifer be damned.*

Suddenly the earth began to rumble. Kenya held on to Darrin as they looked for the source.

A ten-year-old boy, his hands in a tight fist yelled, "Get away from me!"

The ground began to shake again as people ran about, screaming in fear. A nearby water hydrant burst, shooting up like Old Faithful in Yellowstone Park. Then it did something strange, the stream moved to the left, dousing the officers and military members trying to talk to the angry, frightened ten-year-old boy with black hair, his brown eyes glowing.

Kenya noticed a girl who looked to be around twelve or thirteen, holding her hands out. Her brown eyes were glowing as well. She was controlling the water spray. Once the officers were free of their weapons, the girl stopped the water flow and ran to the boy. She hugged him and said, "it will be okay, don't be scared. I won't let them hurt you."

Kenya and Darrin quickly moved toward them, their hands in the air. "We want to help you, please, stay calm," Kenya said. "Let's get you someplace safe before more officers come." Kenya reached her hand to the girl who stood protectively in front of her brother.

"Like you helped those twins, no thanks lady! You gonna shoot me and my brother because of what we can do?" the girl asked.

"No, we want to protect you from the ones who do."

"Kenya," Darrin whispered, "the officers are getting up, let's move!" Kenya nodded looking to the girl for her response.

The girl looked at the men behind Kenya and Darrin and looked to her brother before taking Kenya's hand. "I know a shortcut home," she said.

"Lead the way," Darrin said with a smile, hoping it would calm the two children. Kenya said a few words of prayer and quickly anointed the children with oil. "For protection," she whispered.

The people and officers around them became confused and no longer focused on Kenya, Darrin or the kids with them. They could walk past the officers, paramedics, firefighters and the military personnel who drove away with the twin girls. No one seemed to notice them at all.

Darrin wondered how Kenya could do that and why she had not done that with the twin girls? They cut through the dense forest like trees that surrounded the eleven acre park and came out to a residential area. The street was Jefferson Chase Circle. They entered the backyard of the one the brick houses. Darrin closed the wooden gate behind them, checking the perimeter to see if anyone had spotted them. The backyard was private, nicely kept up they stacked though fallen leaves in a corner near the house.

Once inside the house, everyone gathered in the living room which had modest furniture. The girl called her other siblings and two younger children came in and sat on the couch. Darrin sat quietly in the easy chair and Kenya, preferring to stand, stood next to him.

"There are four of us," the girl began. "I'm Alma Hernandez, the eldest. I'm twelve."

The boy spoke next. "I'm Adan and I'm ten." He pointed to the two younger ones on the couch. "That's Alejo, he's seven and Abril, she's six."

Kenya and Darrin introduced themselves to the children. She studied each one for a moment, she could feel the pulsing energy from each child. "You all have abilities, don't you?" She asked. The children nodded.

"When did they start?" Kenya asked, deciding she would sit after all. This could take a while. She sat on the love seat facing the couch where the children sat looking wide eyed at her and Darrin.

Alma, the eldest girl answered, "for the little ones yesterday, me and Adan have had ours for a few months. It took some practicing, but I think we have better control now. I just told Abril and Alejo not to touch anything and stay in their rooms until I could bring Adan back. Actually, our whole family has some abilities, but my parents said it rarely happens until the teenage years, but something is effecting us now."

"Are your parents witches?" Darrin interjected. "Yes, Alma smiled and blushed. She thought Darrin was really handsome. Darrin smiled back and then turned to Kenya. "Well This your area of expertise, I've got nothing."

Kenya began to tell the children of her own abilities and who she and Darrin worked for. "Where are your parents?" Kenya asked.

"Our father is at work. Our mother just went to run some errands and talk to our *curandera*, Memia Sanchez, but she should be back soon."

"What's a cur-ren-dara?" Darrin asked. "Coo-ran-dare-ra, Kenya corrected, "they are healers, a spiritual doctor," Kenya explained.

"Got it," Darrin said. *Just how many types of witches are there?* He wondered.

"Go ahead Alma, you were saying," Kenya smiled. Alma nodded. "We are home schooled and supposed to be doing our lessons on the computer, but our dog, Rosie, got out. That's why Adan left the house, to go find her."

"And did he?" Darrin asked.

"No," Adan said sadly.

"Sorry bud, tell you what, why don't we go and see if we can find her while my partner talks to your sister. How does that sound?" Darrin still was not comfortable with witchcraft of any sort, save for Kenya's ways and methods. It was really just a way to get out of the house.

Adan's eyes lit up as he nodded yes, "I'll get her leash!"

"I wanna go too," Alejo said.

Kenya wasn't sure it was a good idea given the situation, but relented after Darrin looked at her with pleading eyes, his hands raised to his chest as if he were praying as he mouthed the word, 'please'. She repeated the chant she said earlier along with a prayer and anointed Alejo with van van oil. "Be careful," she said.

"Of course, besides, we're invisible now, right?" Darrin winked at her.

"Something like that," she smiled. Adan grabbed Darrin's hand, "let's go!" The three males headed out the front door as Kenya turned her attention back to the girls.

Two

Kenya learned more about the Hernandez family of witches from Alma and Abril. Each of them had powers pertaining to the elements. Alma could control water, all liquids, even blood. Her brother Adan could move the earth and make plants, even trees, grow. Their younger brother, Alejo, controlled fire, it came not from him, he could only manipulate it, make it bigger, hotter or extinguish it altogether.

When the children's mother, Eva came home, Kenya introduced herself and told her what happened with the children.

"*Aye dios mio, hijos mios*!" (Oh my God, my children!) She said in exasperation. She had been panicking on the drive home when she saw all the emergency vehicles around Empire Park. It took her thirty minutes just to get through to her street. She hugged the girls and fussed at Alma in Spanish for not keeping a better watch on Adan. "*Donde estan mis chicos?* (where are the boys?)" She asked

Kenya while patting her youngest daughter on the head. *"Están con mi compañero Darrin, buscando a Rosie,"* Kenya replied. She was fluent in both Spanish and French. *"Aye dios mio,* that dog! She is always getting out, I told Angel to fix that fence, *pero* she keeps digging!" Eva said as she smoothed back the soft tendrils of hair that escaped her messy bun at the back of her head.

She was an attractive Latina woman, thirty-five years old, a stay-at-mom and a practicing *bruja.* She, like her older children, could move water and earth, while her husband, Angel, could manipulate fire and air. Eva was a petite woman with a curvaceous body and large breasts that strained the top two buttons of her rather modest looking blue sweater. Her husband Angel was a construction worker who was part owner with his cousin, Rafael Ramos, of a company called R & H Construction.

Kenya was just about to ask what kind of dog Rosie was when Darrin and Eva's boys came in the door, a large German Shepard leading the way. Rosie barked wagging her tail and ran to Alma, who began to pet and hug her.

"Darrin, this is Eva Hernandez, the children's mother. Eva, this is my partner, Darrin Selinsky," Kenya said after a few moments. Darrin beamed as he extended his hand to Eva. Eva shook his hand admiring him, *"Mucho gusto. El es muy guapo!*" she said to Kenya. Darrin, who didn't speak Spanish beyond Mexican food, looked to Kenya to translate.

"She says you're very handsome." Kenya crossed her arms and laughed.

"Well, thank you kindly ma'am, you look 'mooy wapo' yourself," Darrin said with a half bow, his southern accent slightly more exaggerated for Eva's sake. It earned him a wide smile from Eva, "*muchas gracias.*"

"Mama," Alma interrupted.

"What *Mija*? I can admire a handsome man, right? *Aye dios mios chica!* You and Adan go get the rest of the groceries from the car for me, OK?" She smiled at her daughter. Alma shook her head as she and Adan went out to the car.

Eva turned back to Darrin and Kenya and thanked them both for getting the children and the dog back home safely.

"Not a problem Mrs. Hernandez. I placed a protection spell on the kids, but you really should be careful, I saw two kids dragged away by the military to God knows where and only He knows what for. You have my number, so call me if you need me. You have a great family and I want to make sure we protect them," Kenya said with concern.

Eva reached out and hugged Kenya, "*muchas gracias senorita.*"

The top of her head came to Kenya's breast and Darrin stirred with excitement watching the two women hug. He tried to keep it to himself as he shifted uneasily in his jeans. They said their goodbyes to the children and Eva promised to keep the kids close and out of the public eye.

Darrin and Kenya took the long way around the streets as they walked back to Empire Park where Darrin's truck sat near the tennis courts. It was late afternoon and Darrin suggested they go get something to eat before heading back to the office.

"Soul food?" Kenya suggested.

"Nah, I think I want some tacos now!" He teased.

"You're so wrong for that!"

They both laughed and Darrin pulled Kenya in for kiss. It was a warm soft kiss, and just what Kenya needed as it was freezing outside. It was December and most, if not all, of the houses had beautiful Christmas lights. Darrin kept his arm around her, mindful of his service weapon, a black Glock 17M, holstered on his hip.

Three

DeKalb County

Thirteen-year-old twins, Justin and Jace Gawain were very smart boys. They were also excellent athletes in middle school, playing football and basketball. Light-skinned with reddish brown hair, dark brown eyes and dimples like their mother, they were very handsome. In fact, they made some boys jealous and the girls flocked around them at school competing for their attention.

The boys were getting off the school bus when another boy behind them threw a football hitting Jace in the back of the head.

"On god, who threw dat?" he yelled.

The boy who threw the ball just laughed and threw his hands up like, 'What?'

Justin, angry that someone hit his brother, picked up the ball and threw it at the boy, hitting him in the stomach and knocking him hard against the bus. Everyone gasped, including Jace. There was a dent in the bus's side where the boy landed. Justin was strong, but not that strong.

"Oops, my bad, but I barely threw it." Justin said. He was just as shocked as everyone else. He hoped the kid was not hurt.

The boy, named Aaron, crippled by the pain in his back stumbled as he tried to stand. "Ow, ow, can somebody call my mom?" Tears welled and threatened to fall.

Jace began to panic worrying that his brother would get into big trouble because Aaron looked seriously hurt. He wished that it had not happened at all. He closed his eyes and balled his fists.

When he opened his eyes, he and his brother were getting off the bus again and he felt the football hit his head. *What the...?*

Jace quickly picked up the ball with his left hand and looked at his brother. "It's ok Justin, I'm good, dude."

Justin shook his head. *Deja vu? What is going on?*

Jace handed the ball back to Aaron, "it was just an

accident, right?"

Aaron looked surprised, but took the ball. "Yeah whatever, dude," he said as he walked across the street to his house.

Justin pulled Jace close to him. "What was that? One minute I hurt him and now he's fine!" he whispered.

"I don't know dude. I mean, I just wished it had not happened, I was scared and..."

"Did you make it so what I did doesn't happen?" Justin whispered.

"I guess, but what about you? You were like superman or something! You dented the side of the bus!"

"I don't know!" Justin yelled as suddenly everything around them stopped. No wind, no sound, people stopped in their tracks and cars were no longer moving. Time stood still except for Justin and Jace.

He gulped as he looked around. His heart beat fast and he began to sweat. *What's happening to me?*

"Justin, how did you do that?

"I don't know, but we gotta get home dude, like now!"

And just like that, they found themselves at the front

door of their house and everyone started to move again. The boys quickly ran inside. "Mom!" they yelled in unison.

Danae Gawain, their mom, was making them a snack in the kitchen as the boys ran to her gripping her around her waist.

"What the hell is wrong with y'all? I almost cut myself with the butter knife!" she fussed.

"Ah, sorry ma," Justin muttered.

"Yeah, uh sorry mama," Jace whispered.

Danae was about to fuss again, but the look on her son's faces told her something was wrong.

Danae was a beautiful plus sized, light-skinned black woman with short dreadlocked dark brown hair and brown eyes. When she smiled, her deep set dimples added to her beauty.

"Is somebody gonna to tell me what's going on?" she asked with a frown.

Justin spoke up first. "Ma, I know this is gonna sound crazy, but I think I just stopped time!"

"Yeah and I turned it back!" Jace interjected.

Danae smiled with relief. "Oh, is that all? I thought y'all did something wrong! Don't scare me like that!"

Jace and Justin looked at each and then back at their mom. "What do you mean, 'is that all'?" they said together.

"I was gonna wait for your daddy to sit you both down and tell you before your 13th birthday, but we were all so busy, and since nothing happened for months after your birthday, I thought maybe it wouldn't happen until next year."

"Can you tell us now then? Daddy won't be back until tomorrow and I am not going anywhere until I know what is happening to me. If Jace hadn't turned back time, I was going to juvie for sure! I threw a ball at Aaron because he hit Jace on the back of his head with it and I got mad. The ball hit him so hard, it threw him into the side of the school bus and left a big dent!" Justin said.

"Oh my god! Well, get your snacks and let's sit at the kitchen table." Danae answered.

Once they were all seated at the table, Danae began, "Our family is special. We are not witches or anything like that, but we have certain 'gifts.' I wasn't sure what your gifts would be, but I thought since you Justin, were always so fast, impatient, and always rushing, I thought you could speed up or stop time like my dad. Jace, you are a bit slower and don't handle change well, so it makes sense that you can reset time or rather, rewind it."

"Can you do that too, Mama? Jace asked as he bit into his peanut butter and jelly sandwich.

"No, mine is very different. I can see spirits, the ones that just died hours or even days ago. I can absorb energy, like electricity, and zap people," she laughed.

"No wonder you always shocked us! I just thought you rubbed your feet on the carpet!" Jace laughed. He felt a little better knowing their family was special.

Danae continued to explain about their gifts and that she would ask her dad to help train the boys. When they were born, their grandfather called them "skip and rewind", but now Danae understood what he meant. Justin's strength surprised her though, that was not a gift any of her family members had.

Jace went to pick up his cup, but it floated up instead. He scared him and when he jumped back; The glass crashed to the table in pieces. "Ah, sorry ma! I don't..." he started to say.

"It's alright, I guess that's your second gift. You can

move things without touching them. I guess lots of things will break now." Danae smiled.

Jace was expecting to get yelled at, but his mom cleaned the apple juice from the table and the broken glass pieces without another word.

Justin and Jace looked at each. Jace shrugged. Justin just shook his head. Neither one could explain why their mom didn't fuss, but Justin was going to take full advantage of her good mood.

"So ma, can we play basketball until dinner and then do our homework?"

"Yeah, I guess so, just be careful, take it easy on Jace. No using your powers!"

"I'll try!" Justin grinned.

Jace gave Justin a wide-eyed look. "Don't worry, mama, I can handle him!"

"Maybe!" Justin teased.

They walked out the front door to the basketball hoop in the driveway.

Danae washed the dishes and then sat down in the living room to watch television.

"Breaking news... several children and a few adults were injured after a set of twin girls with supernatural powers attacked them today in Empire Park..."

Danae's eyes went wide with fear as she witnessed the girls being tranquilized and taken away. Her worst nightmare was coming true. The world may have accepted witchcraft along with psychic powers, but active powers was something else. In fear for her boys, she called Kenya Clark. She and Kenya had known each other since high school and if anyone could help, she could.

"Hey Danae, what's up? I'm heading back to work."

"Kenya, I just saw you on the news and well, my boys just got their powers today, is something going on? Where are they taking those little girls?"

"Oh no! Of all the days for them to get their powers, it just had to be today! I don't know where they are taking those girls, but it can't be good. Has something happened over there?"

"Yeah, as they got off the bus, but Jace shifted time back like it didn't happen. I just don't know if anyone felt or sensed a *deja vu*."

"Well damn, that explains why Darren and I crossed

the same street twice. Where are the boys now?" Kenya asked. Only those with special gifts can sense if there has been a shift or repeat of time.

"They went outside, but I will tell them to come in."

"Ok, sit tight. I will make a couple phone calls and head over. Keep the boys *inside*, alright?" Kenya said.

"Ok, just please hurry. See ya when you get here." Danae said before hanging up.

The second call she made was to her husband Carl, an over-the-road truck diver, and actually on his way home sooner than expected. She told him what happened with the twin girls in Empire Park earlier and with their boys.

Carl said he was about 45 minutes out, but may be delayed with traffic. "Don't panic Danae, it's gonna be alright. We'll keep the boys safe and I'm sure Kenya will help us." Carl said to comfort his wife.

"Alright baby, just get here soon, ok?" Danae said sadly.

They boys were playing one on one when Aaron and two other boys, Ronald and Davis, came to the driveway.

"Hey Jace, can we play?" Aaron asked.

Justin had the ball, but stopped dribbling when the

boys came up. He looked at Jace nervously.

"Ah, well me and Justin are playing, so maybe tomorrow. We have to go in soon to do our homework." Jace said. Aaron had never come over to hang out with them before so Jace was a little more than suspicious.

"Ah c'mon man, what's the matter? You sacred we gonna beat you or something?"

"I ain't never scared, man! But Jace is right. We have homework to do," Justin replied.

"So maybe you da one scared, huh Justin? Come get this ass whoopin!" Aaron laughed as he rushed toward Justin. The other two boys went after Jace.

Three against two, the boys fought in the front yard. Justin spun and flipped Aaron, pinning him quickly and began punching him in his face. After three or four blows, he stopped and got off Aaron backing away from him in horror. Blood squirted as Aaron turned his head to spit out his tooth. His face was bloody.

Jace defended himself against the two boys, but Ronald grabbed his arms and held him fast as Davis began punching him in the stomach. Jace barely had time to catch his breath before yelling for his brother. Justin immediately went for Davis, knocking him to the ground hard and breaking his right forearm as he hit the ground.

"Ow, damn! Ok, ok!" Davis cried. His arm began to swell and bruise.

Justin got up and looked at Davis." I'm sorry, but you need to lay off my brother!"

Ronald let go of Jace and shoved him to the ground, he was about to go after Justin when he felt a shock hit his body like someone had hit him with a taser. He fell to the ground shaking and wetting himself.

Jace looked up to see his mother with her hand outstretched. "Boys, get in the house now!" she said.

Justin helped Jace stand up and without a word, they ran in the house, too scared to use their powers. They had never seen their mother shock anyone before. It both impressed and scared them at the same time.

Danae looked at the boys who attacked her sons as they lay in her driveway with no empathy. Her neighbors watched her, their eyes were wide with fear.

"Somebody call the police! This witch attacked these boys!" someone yelled.

"Call the police, bitch! Those boys came after *my*

sons! I defend mine! Ain't no law against that and I ain't no witch!" Danae screamed back at her neighbors.

When the police and several ambulances came on the scene, they found Danae sitting on a bench on her front porch, arms folded.

"Officers, there she is, she hurt those boys, don't let her lie to you! I saw her tase him!" An angry female neighbor shouted.

"Kiss my ass Cindy, I don't even have a taser!" Danae yelled back as she walked over to the injured boys on her property.

Another person shouted, "No, it was her hands. She has powers!"

Four paramedics and a male officer approached Danae, "Ma'am can you step back please and let the paramedics do their job?"

Danae muttered to herself as she stepped away from the boys. *Kenya, where are you?*

Suddenly, everything went still, the angry neighbors, police, paramedics, even the three injured boys on the ground. However, Danae could move and she turned to see her son, Justin standing on the porch just outside the front door, a tear slid down his cheek and he quickly wiped it away.

"I don't want you to go to jail, Mama," he said.

Danae walked over to him and hugged him. "I'm not. Auntie Kenya will help, you'll see. Let them go now, baby."

Justin swallowed hard as his brother came outside. "I can reverse it Mama," Jace said.

"No baby, too much time has passed and you are just learning how to use your power. It's gonna be okay. Trust me."

"Ok, Mama," Jace said as he took her right hand in his.

"Let them go Justin, it's okay."

Justin took a deep breath and released it slowly. Everyone moved again as if nothing had happened.

Four

Deputy Director Daniel Michaels arrived at the Gawain residence along with two agents, Jace Howard and Ligaya Ocampo. Kenya called Daniel asked him to protect her friend, Danae and her family. Daniel brought two agents with him as backup, not knowing what to expect.

Agent Howard is a handsome dark-skinned man with dark brown eyes. His muscular and broad shoulder frame draped by the suit he wore did little to hide his well-defined, less than eight percent body fat, physique. He is exceptional in marksmanship and all weapons, including hand to hand combat.

His partner at work and at home, Special Agent Ligaya Ocampo is a Filipino witch or *bruha*, a former *mangkukulam*, who practiced Kulam, a form of folk magic to curse and trick others. However, after meeting Jace,

Ligaya changed her ways and is now more of a healer, an *albularyo*. Her small, five foot four frame with a tiny waist, fools many who think her weak. A master martial artist in four forms, she is an excellent fighter.

She is strong both physically and spiritually. A true beauty inside and out with her dark brown almond-shaped eyes and waist long, silky black hair.

When they first arrived on the street, everything was still. People were frozen in place like statues, birds were perfectly still in mid-flight. Agent Howard was a bit freaked out as he drove down the street to the Gawain residence.

"What kind of magic is this?" he asked.

"None that I have seen. Still, someone is doing this and that's why we are here," Agent Ocampo said.

"Witches can do this?"

"Not where I come from. This is stronger. I don't think this is witchcraft at all. It's not malevolent, but powerful. Wait, look, the woman and the two boys, they're still moving; it must be one of them." Agent Ligaya pointed out.

"That's the Gawain place right?"

"Yeah," Agent Ocampo said verifying the address on her

phone.

Director Michaels was in the car behind them as they parked across the street from the house. It doesn't bother him to see this, but if Kenya wanted this family protected, he now knew why. By the time he parked his truck, got out and walked toward the woman and her sons, everyone was moving again.

"Danae Gawain?" he asked as he approached the woman and her two boys.

"Yes," Danae replied.

"I'm Director Daniel Michaels, Kenya's boss. She sent me to you. She is on her way though." he smiled.

"Oh, ok, good," Danae said with a smile of relief. "These are my sons, Justin and Jace."

"Nice to meet you," Daniel said extending his hand to Justin.

The boys nodded and kept their hands at their side. Daniel withdrew his hand. He did not take offense; He figured the situation terrified the boys enough and he is a stranger to them.

"Don't be rude boys, he's here to help!" Danae elbowed Justin.

"Ow! Sorry, uh nice to meet you," Justin said, his hands still at his side.

"Yeah, me too," Jace said.

Agents Howard and Ocampo walked up and stood next to Daniel.

"Are they with you too?" Danae asked.

"Yes, this is Special Agent Jace Howard and Special Agent Ligaya Ocampo." Daniel introduced. Both agents smiled and nodded their heads.

"Hey, my name is Jace too!" Jace smiled at Agent Howard.

"Oh well, that makes us twins then! Nice to meet ya!" Agent Howard exclaimed as he shook Jace's hand.

"Which one of you made everything freeze?" Agent Ocampo asked.

"Ah, before you answer that, let's talk inside. If that is alright Mrs. Gawain?" Daniel said with a quick side eye at Ligaya.

"Yeah, come on in," Danae said and led them inside the house as the paramedics put the injured boys into the ambulances.

"Ah, excuse me, but I need to take Mrs. Gawain in for

questioning and get her statement." Officer Fisher said.

Daniel flashed his credentials. "I'm the Deputy Director of the GBI. We'll be taking it from here. If your sergeant has a problem, here's my card."

Officer Fisher took the card. "Alright then, I will just get the statements from the witnesses.

"Whatever you need to do. I will send someone to collect those later." Daniel said smugly.

Officer Fisher did not like when federal agents of any kind came in and took over their cases. However, to him, this incident seemed pretty normal and not supernatural. Boys fighting in the yard, the mom comes out with a taser to protect her sons, nothing unusual about that at all. *So why is the GBI here?* He thought to himself. Odd that they would show up and *when* had they arrived? He did not remember them coming up. One minute, he was just talking to the woman and the next; she was talking to two men and woman. He shrugged it off and reluctantly; He went back to interview the people standing around in the street.

Danae led her sons and the GBI agents inside and offered them coffee. Daniel and Agent Howard took her offer and Agent Ocampo asked for a glass of water. Jace thought Agent Ocampo was pretty and so he volunteered to bring her water.

After everyone was seated in the living room, Danae explained that she and her children had certain 'gifts' that were in fact inherited. She also told them that the boys just manifested their gifts today. The agents listened intently with great curiosity. This was way beyond their understanding of the supernatural.

Daniel knew that Kenya inherited her gifts, but stopping time, rewinding it, super strength, and telekinesis were so much more. He did not want to see this family taken away and split up to be studied somewhere or used as weapons. Just then, the front door opened and Carl walked in.

"Daddy! I thought you weren't coming back until tomorrow!" the boys yelled in unison.

Danae gave her husband a big smile that showed her deep dimples.

"No, I'm home!" Carl said as he hugged his wife and kids.

Danae was introducing Carl to the agents when there was a knock at the door. Everyone gasped as if expecting the worse.

"Danae, it's Kenya and Darrin," Kenya said through the door.

Danae opened the door and nearly knocked Kenya over as she hugged her friend. Daniel pulled the agents aside including Darrin who walked over to Agent Jace and shook his hand, leaving Kenya and Danae talking in hushed tones.

"I'm so glad you are here! Today has been rough!" Danae said.

"Yeah, so many kids are manifesting powers that the city is in an uproar about what to do. I think the NSA or some other government group may try to round them up. But, don't you worry about the boys, my dad has a cabin in the mountains in North Georgia. It has three bedrooms on five acres and its secluded so the boys can develop their powers. It's too risky to stay here." Kenya told Danae, hoping she would not be too stubborn or proud to take the cabin.

"Wait, what about Carl's job?" Danae asked.

"Woman, I can drive from anywhere! It don't matter where we live!" Carl said as he stepped closer to his wife and Kenya. His handsome face looked worried. He didn't care where they went as long as his family was safe.

"Ok Kenya, what do we need to do?" Danae asked.

"Pack your bags, take only what you need. I'll call my dad and let him know the situation." Kenya assured her.

"What about school?" Jace chimed in.

"For now, home school may be just what you need until you get your powers under control." Kenya replied.

"Why can't we just go to school up there?" Justin asked, upset at the thought of leaving his friends and his team.

"Baby, until you control your powers, it's just too risky," Danae explained.

"Aw man, I want to play in the championship game! I don't wanna be stuck in a cabin with bears and mountain lions!" Jace exclaimed.

"It's gonna be fine, we will be together and safe, that's all that matters." Carl said as he touched Jace's shoulder. Jace nodded.

"I'll need your cell phones, don't want anyone tracking you. We can get you new ones, maybe even radios. No landline at the cabin." Kenya said.

The boys groaned and so did Danae, but they handed over their phones. Then Jace and Justin went to their rooms to pack. Kenya took out the sim cards and destroyed the phones just as Daniel, Agents Jace, Ligaya and Darren walked over to them.

"Kenya, we need to get the Gawain family to a safe house.

I can coordinate with the FBI and use one of theirs." Daniel began.

"It's all settled Chief, they are going to our cabin in the Georgia mountains. A government safe house is the last place they need to be. Especially if the government is rounding up anyone with powers right now." Kenya explained.

"Good idea, Clark. Jace, why don't you and Ligaya go with them and stay as extra protection." Daniel said.

"For how long, sir?" Agent Ocampo asked.

"Until further notice. I don't want anyone there that I don't trust. Think of this as a little work vacation. But no one, and I mean, *no one*, can know you are there, got it?"

"Got it sir," Agent Ocampo said.

"No problem sir, we're on it." Agent Howard agreed.

"Kenya, I need you and Darren in town, we need to find out where they are taking the twin girls and others that are being taken. Why don't we all meet back at Theo's place in two hours? That will give everyone time to pack and do what they need to before they go." Daniel said.

"But sir, I would prefer to go with Danae..."

"I know she's your friend, but that is precisely why I want

you to stay here. You are too close to this. That's an order."

"Yes, Chief," Kenya said sadly. She knew he was right.

"Kenya, they will be fine, we'll guard them with our lives, okay?" Agent Ocampo assured her.

"You better!" Kenya winked. She knew they were both skilled agents and could handle their own, especially against anyone the government may try to send. Besides, she needed to find out how and why Lucious was involved and try to protect others, he may affect.

Kenya called her dad, and after a quick breakdown of the situation, Theo agreed to everything, even volunteering himself and Reina to take them up there.

Five

Lucious / Lucifer

"So far, things are going according to plan, master," Simaal, one of the higher ranking demons, reported to Lucifer. To everyone in the law firm, he was Simon Cheatham, attorney-at-law, one partner in Lucious Morningside's law firm, Morningside, Dewey, Cheatham, and Howe. A recent addition to Atlanta's list of prestigious law firms.

"Yes, indeed they are. I love the smell of chaos and human suffering!" Lucifer smiled sitting at his desk in his high rise office in midtown Atlanta. His light blue eyes shone brilliantly, a stark contrast to his medium brown skin. Though he can appear as anyone, he chose to appear as a very handsome African American male named Lucious Morningside, impeccably groomed in an Alexander Amosu Vanquish II Bespoke suit. They make one of the most expensive suits in the world from rare vicuna and qivuik wool in a black pinstripe. With nine buttons made of pure 18 carat gold and diamonds, there was enough bling and any other jewelry would be almost too much. He paired it with a white button dress shirt and a pure silk tie in light blue to match his eyes.

"Have they activated all the demon seeds in Atlanta?"

"Not all, my Lord. Would you like me to activate the last two in metro Atlanta?"

"The more the merrier! One big happy family wouldn't you say?" Lucious chuckled.

"Oh, yes, indeed! I will get right on it, sir!" Simaal's violet eyes sparkled. He would do anything to keep his master happy. With a deep bow, he left Lucious' office.

Lucious opened his laptop, struck a few keys, and Kenya appeared on screen. No need for a crystal ball in this modern age. Kenya looked worried and tense. He watched intently wanting to know her, wishing he could appeal to her to in some way. She was part of his bloodline. His daughter Raagna may be gone, but Kenya is still around and he wants her for himself. However, Darrin was always around whenever he spied on her. *Doesn't he ever leave? I need to get rid of him!*

I know, I will send someone to break them up! She couldn't possibly like everything about him! I know just who I need!

He pushed a button on his phone and instantly, he began to facetime a beautiful demon who appeared on his screen.

"Yes Zaddy... I mean, *Master*, how may I serve you?" she said seductively, smiling sweetly and licking her full lips with her forked tongue as her tail swished behind her. Her copper skin glowed and her yellow-green eyes with long dark lashes winked at Lucifer. Her long, shiny black hair in thick braids down her back. Her wings are the softest of any other succubus demon, resembling the feathers of a crow.

"Lissa, my sweet succubus child, I have a job for you. I need you to seduce Darrin Selinsky. Find out as much as you can about him and get him away from my progeny,

Kenya Clark!"

"Anything for you, *Master*," she cooed.

"Report back to me as soon as you can!" he ordered.

Lissa winked again and blew him a kiss before the screen went black.

"Well, that takes care of him," Lucious sighed. Lissa was one of his best succubi. If anyone could get to Darrin, she could. He made some more calls and then settled back in his chair. Night had fallen and he turned to look out the glass window at the city.

Taking a long look at the buildings, he smiled to himself as he watched the shadows. The demons lurking in the night around the houses and businesses decorated with Christmas lights. The sounds of the emergency sirens going back and forth. The sounds of people arguing, fighting, killing, lying, crying, stealing and screwing.

I will never understand Father, why you adore these creatures. So easily manipulated, they adore you one minute and curse you the next. Humans, how the hell did they become your most beloved creation? Well, look at them now. Worthless, ungrateful bastards.

He spun around to face his desk, poured himself a

glass of Merlot and took a sip enjoying the rich aroma and taste. *Maybe they are good for some things.*

Six

Kenya's Place

Darrin walked Kenya to her door. It had been a long day and they were both tired, but all Darrin wanted was to be with Kenya. Stopping at her door, he pulled her in for a kiss. The kiss deepened.

Kenya pulled away. "Want to come inside?"

"I thought you'd never ask," Darrin whispered as he took the keys from Kenya and unlocked the door. Then he lifted her up and carried her inside, kicking the door closed behind them.

Silver stretched lazy on his corner of the couch and opened his eyes. He watched as Darrin carried Kenya to her bedroom then he curled back up for another cat nap.

Darrin placed gently on the bed as he continued to devour her mouth, moving to her neck before he pulled her sweater over head. Removing her blouse and bra, he hungrily sucked her nipples, sending waves of pleasure through her body.

Kenya ran her fingers through his hair, pulling as another wave swept through her. Darrin released just long enough to remove his own clothing as she slid down her pants and panties. Pushing her legs open, Darrin licked her warm center and within moments, brought her screaming the first of her orgasms of the night. Darrin loved the gush of warm liquid that spilled from her. It excited him even more each time.

Giving her a few seconds to recover, he then thrust himself between her legs reveling in the soft, warm hold she had on him. Kenya writhed and hoisted her hips up as another orgasm began to build, her moans becoming louder as her passion built to a crescendo that overflowed into her as she spilled her essence again, tightening and pulsing around his member.

Darrin could barely hold back his release, but wanted to make sure Kenya had all she wanted before he spilled himself inside her. Sweat glistened on his body as he thrust twice more and then released. His eyes glowed and so did Kenya's. They looked at each in awe. Their bodies began to glow, Kenya's had a yellow glow while Darrin had almost a neon blue color. They felt weightless and it was then that they noticed they were hovering over the bed, almost to the ceiling!

Neither knew what was happening. Darrin held Kenya fast. She was beautiful, her legs wrapped around his waist and her arms around his neck. He kissed her neck and closed his eyes, willing them into a slow descent onto the bed.

"What was that?" Kenya asked after a few moments.

"I don't know, that is definitely a first!" he answered.

"Is it your power or mine?"

"Not sure. Whatever it is, I'm not complaining!" he laughed.

"It was definitely amazing! I think it's you; you have angel blood. With all the extra powers floating around, I think you just got an extra boost!"

"I probably needed it, but you are glowing too, so maybe its a combination of us together. For a minute there, I thought we were flying!"

"Maybe you can!"

"Maybe... but right now, I just want stay right where I am, here with you. I love you, Kenya."

Kenya swallowed hard. That was the first time he said that and she felt the same. "I love you too, Darrin," she beamed. She moved to kiss him gently as Darrin's heat beat a little faster. He had been wanting to say that for months now, but he never felt it more than he did right now.

Kenya was not completely over Daniel, but Darrin held her heart now and she was not about to walk away from that. She would always love Daniel, but not in the way she loved Darrin. They pretty much all got along now, things stopped being awkward during Thanksgiving at her dad's house. Darrin and Daniel actually bonded. Suddenly she had a thought.

"Darrin, we should go see your dad tomorrow. I don't think he's telling you everything. I could be wrong, but I feel it pretty strongly."

"What made you think of that?"

"Well, your power boost for one and two, I would really like to know if I am dating a real angel," she giggled.

"Well, you've got demon blood, so I guess I am dating a demon. Opposites attract, right? But yeah, if you feel this strongly about it, let's do it. I trust your instincts so I will call my Daddy in the morning."

"Ok, good," she yawned and nuzzled closer to him, closing her eyes. He stroked her arm gently before falling into a deep sleep.

He dreamed of Kenya, but her kisses were different. She did not smell like Kenya or even feel like her. It was Kenya's face and body, even her voice, but not Kenya. *What the hell?* Darrin woke with a start.

He looked over at Kenya, sleeping peacefully on his chest. Just a crazy a dream. He kissed the top of Kenya's head and went back to sleep, oblivious of the succubus that hovered over the bed. With a haughty laugh, Lissa disappeared into the night.

Seven

David and Alice Selinsky

Darrin was never really that close to his father, but this was too important to ignore. His father, David Selinsky, had been courteous enough over the phone and agreed to let Darrin and Kenya come over. Darrin wanted Kenya to meet his parents anyway and now was as good a time as any.

He hoped they would welcome Kenya, but he really wasn't sure. His last serious girlfriend left with most of his savings, and he had brought no one else to meet David and Alice Selinsky. He suddenly wished he had a better relationship with his parents, like Kenya and her dad, Theo, seemed to have.

Darrin held Kenya's hand and gave it squeeze as he knocked on the door of his parent's home. His mother answered the door. She was short with medium length blonde hair pulled back into a bun. Her green eyes danced with excitement at seeing her son. Kenya now knew where Darrin's beautiful eyes came from.

"Darrin, what in the world? I didn't know you were comin' with company! Lord, I must look a fright!" she smiled at him feeling embarrassed by stained pullover sweater and jeans. She yanked the blue handkerchief she had tied over her blond hair off and smoothed her hair back. She was cleaning the house like she did every Saturday for the last forty years.

"You look fine mama, but I guess Daddy didn't tell you I was coming. I am not surprised." Darrin said dryly.

"Well, you know your father, he never says much anyway about anything. Come on in son, it's too cold out there," she motioned and stepped back so Darrin and Kenya could come inside.

The house was small, but cozy and spotless, Kenya noticed. The décor was modest, but the Christmas decorations looked like something you would find on Pinterest or Etsy.

Once inside, Darrin introduced Kenya. "Mama, this is Special Agent Kenya Clark, my partner and my girlfriend," he beamed as he winked at Kenya.

"Kenya, this is my mama, Alice Selinsky."

"Oh, my goodness! Well, aren't you just a doll! I am so pleased to meet you!" Alice beamed and moved to give Kenya a big hug. Kenya was surprised, but more than happy to hug her back. She smelled like lemons and her hug was warm and welcoming.

"It's nice to meet you Mrs. Selinsky," Kenya smiled.

"Oh Darrin, she is just beautiful! Please make yourself at home while I get your father out here. David! Darrin is here and his girlfriend is just as pretty as she can be!" Alice yelled as she walked down the hall to the master bedroom.

"Wow, your mom is so sweet baby. Why were you so worried?" Kenya teased.

"It's not her I am worried about." Darrin sighed, but smiled at Kenya. Though glad his mother seemed to take to Kenya, he was pretty sure his dad would not be as welcoming.

Alice returned to the living room with David and promptly sat on the sofa. Darrin and Kenya stood up.

"Good to see ya Daddy, ah this is Special..."

"Well, this one is good looking, but are you sure she

is who she says she is? Is she a witch too?" David grumbled, interrupting his son.

"Daddy, don't start! She works with me, she's an agent. Special Agent Kenya Clark and no, she's not a witch." Darrin replied, his anger beginning to rise. Kenya stepped in front and thrust her hand to David.

"Nice to meet Mr. Selinsky, Darrin has told me a lot about you," she smiled.

"Well, I've heard little about you until this morning, but it's nice to meet ya all the same." David muttered, shaking Kenya's hand firmly.

Kenya suddenly saw an elderly woman sitting in a chair alone in a room staring at a television. David felt a jolt from Kenya and tried to pull away, but Kenya gripped him until her vision stopped.

"What in the Sam Hill? I thought you said she wasn't a witch!" David yelled as he felt his fear rising. He could not see what Kenya was seeing, but he felt her power; it unnerved him.

"She's not! She has certain abilities though. She is part of the Paranormal Crimes Investigation Unit of the GBI."

"Cain't you ever date a 'normal' woman?" David

fumed.

"Believe me Daddy, 'normal' is overrated," Darrin replied.

Kenya released David's hand. "Mr. Selinsky, who is Irma Grace?"

"That's my mama, she passed on years ago." David whispered.

"Kenya, what did you see, honey?"

"I'm sorry Darrin, he's lying, your grandma is still alive. She's alone and very sad."

"Daddy, is this true?"

"Ah hell, you gonna believe this..."

"Careful Daddy, this is the woman I love and she has no reason to lie! Her gifts are *very* real!"

"Okay, okay! Everybody just settle down and I'll tell you what's what." David sighed heavily.

"David, you told me she was dead!" Alice exclaimed. She was disappointed, but her frown had little effect on David.

"Not now, Alice. Please, just let me explain." David pleaded as he slumped down in his easy chair. Alice sat down on the sofa next to Kenya and Darrin across from David. All eyes were on him and he began to sweat.

"Your granddaddy is not really your granddaddy, not by blood anyhow. My mama married him when I was three years old. He adopted me and that's how I got the name Selinsky. My mama told my grandma that she slept with an angel and that's how she had me. No one believed her and this 'angel' fella never married my mom. He would visit her from time to time she told me later. Anyway, my grandma tried to keep her quiet about the whole thing, you know back then, folks didn't take to kindly to unwed mamas, you know. My grandparents finally married her off to Derwood Selinsky. He was a humble man whose parents owned a grocery store. He didn't care that she had me. Well, they moved here where no one would question my birth, because no one knew us here. Derwood had blue eyes like mine, so everyone just accepted that he was my daddy. Derwood is my daddy, he raised me. As my mama got older, she would forget things, but she would not forget her 'angel.' She was talking so much about him that folks thought she was ill. My daddy had to put her away. I was in my late teens then, and I used to visit her a lot. She would fill my head with stories that my daddy didn't want me to repeat. She said God blessed me and I had powers, but I never got em. I was ashamed of her after that and I stopped going to see her. I started telling everyone she died and when Daddy died, he left money for me to keep her in that place and that's what I do. Doctors say she's delusional and they keep her calm. I was just so ashamed and I'm sorry son, I kept that from ya. From you too, Alice. Awful sorry." David's eyes filled with tears. His shame washed over him and he cried for the first time in front of his son and his wife.

"Oh honey, it's alright," Alice said. What he said moved her and she went over to him to console him.

Darrin was furious. "When I came to you a couple months back and told you about my power, you said you had no idea how that could have happened! Why did you lie, Daddy, why?"

"It upset me. I realized my mother had been telling the truth and I was… jealous of you! All of this time, I wanted to be special, to be somebody. I'm so sorry, son. I shoulda told ya, my pride just got in the way."

"Daddy, you will always be special to me, but I needed your help you selfish son of a..."

"Darrin, don't you talk to your father like that! I'll not have it! Alice fussed.

"Sorry mama, you're right! I'm sorry, Daddy." Darrin sighed. "Can I see her? Would she be able to talk to me?"

"Yeah, yeah, thank you, son. She's at The Azalea House over in Decatur. I went to see her after you told me what happened to you. She wants to meet you. I'm just so sorry I let pride keep me from telling ya."

Kenya touched Darrin's arm. "Forgive him, he's your dad and dads aren't perfect, but he is the only one you've got."

Darrin nodded. "It's alright Daddy. I don't understand it all, but I accept your apology."

"Thank you son," David sighed. Darrin patted his father on the back. Alice reached to hug her son.

"Go see her today, son and then maybe you both can come over for dinner next week!"

"We would love that mama, thank you. Kenya, would you go with me to see my grandma?" Darrin asked.

"Well, since you're the one driving, and you asked so nicely, sure, I would love to." Kenya smiled.

"Oh, she's a good one, a real keeper." David said.

"Well, I do believe you're right, Daddy. I think I'll keep her!" Darrin teased as he kissed Kenya on the cheek.

"Oh, maybe I can finally look forward to some grandkids! They will be gorgeous!" Alice chimed in.

Kenya's cheeks flushed as everyone laughed and David moved toward Darrin and gave him a hug. Darrin brushed away a tear that spilled down his cheek as he hugged his father.

Eight

Irma Grace

The nursing home seemed pleasant enough as Darrin and Kenya walked hand in hand to the front desk. They signed in and clipped on the visitor badges. When they reached room 184, Darrin knocked on the door.

"Yes?" a voice called out.

"Ms. Irma Grace, It's Darrin Selinsky. I'm your grandson."

"Oh, my Lord! Is that really you, my little angel?" Irma said sweetly.

"Yes ma'am, not so little anymore. Can we come in?"

"Yes, please do."

Darrin and Kenya walked in to find an attractive mature lady sitting in the corner chair dressed in a gray pullover sweater and black pants. Her white medium length hair was in a bob shimmering with silver highlights that captured the light coming from the window. Her face was smooth with very few wrinkles making her look more like she was in her 50s, not her 80s. Her blue-gray eyes lit up the moment she saw Darrin.

"I have waited quite a long time to meet you." she said.

Darrin was unsure if he should shake her hand, kiss her cheek, or give her a big hug. And as if on cue, she stood up ad threw her arms open. "Well, come on, give your grandma a hug!" Irma beamed.

Darrin let go of Kenya's hand and went to Irma for a hug. "It's so good to meet ya... ah... what should I call you?"

"Grandma Grace will do," Irma said with a smile and a wink.

"Grandma Grace... I like it." Darrin said.

"And who is the lovely young woman behind you?"

"Grandma Grace, this is Kenya Clark, my girlfriend and my partner, she's a fellow agent of the GBI and one of the best women I know."

"Delighted, young lady. Come, give me a hug, you're family." Irma squealed.

"Ah, we're not married," Darrin corrected.

"Not yet, my dear. I cannot wait to meet my great granddaughters! Oh dear, I'm getting ahead of myself. Now, come take a seat and ask your questions. I'm sure you have many." Irma laughed sweetly.

Did she say great granddaughters? Kenya thought to herself. She hadn't thought of herself as a mother, but she wasn't opposed to the idea either.

Darrin smiled at Kenya. Irma was the second person to talk about them having children. If one more person says it, it will be official. He could definitely see marrying Kenya and having two little girls who looked like her would be even better. He sighed as he sat down on the love seat across from his grandma.

"So Grandma Grace, who is my real grandfather, and how did you meet?"

"His name is Aliel, well, his celestial name anyway. In human form, he is Alan Fredricks. He was the most beautiful man I've ever seen. I used to dance ballet from the time I was a little girl until the end of my teenage years.

One day when I was twenty years old, I wasn't paying attention and I walked into traffic. A car hit me and the driver took me to the hospital. I'm not sure how long I was out, but I woke up and saw my mama praying at the foot of my bed and behind her was a large bright light. It was blue, I think. I thought maybe it was from the window, but then the light moved and formed the outline of a man. I remember his eyes, they were so blue, like the ocean in the Caribbean. Anyway, the doctors said I would never dance again once I healed. The impact broke my legs from the knees down. I was expecting to be in a wheelchair for the rest of my life. I refused to eat, being a ballerina was all I ever wanted to be. They kept me sedated most of the time for fear I would harm myself. One night, a janitor was emptying trash in the hall and he came in my room to empty my trashcan. When I looked at him, I saw those same blue eyes that I had seen a few days before. He asked me why I wasn't eating and I told him what happened to me. He told me I should stop feeling sorry for myself! That this was not the end of my life and I should not give up. Well, I cussed him out and called him everything but a child of God, but it didn't phase him at all! Night after night, he'd come, we'd talk, laugh, and he healed me. Not just my body, but my heart too..." Irma began to cough, her throat was dry.

"Are you alright?" Darrin asked.

"Some water sweetie, if you don't mind." Irma whispered, her voice hoarse. Kenya motioned to Darrin that she would go and then she left to get Irma some water.

"Is this too much for you? We can come back another time." Darrin asked.

"No, it's fine sweetie," she assured him.

Kenya returned with a glass of water and gave it to Irma.

"Thank you, dear," Irma said before taking a few sips. "Much better. Let's continue. Now, where was I? Oh yes! Aliel healed me and helped me walk again. I was his assignment, you know? He was just supposed to heal me and go back to heaven. He didn't plan on falling in love with me. We spent more and more time together. When we were intimate, he gave me some of his grace, that is how your father came to be."

"Is that also why you look so young?" Kenya asked.

"Oh my goodness, yes! I age much slower, but not slow enough. Although, I may outlive your father at this rate!" Irma laughed.

"Can you tell me what kind of powers I have or expect to have? Why doesn't my dad have power?"

"Well, from what I've been told, your father was not pure enough, he is good, but he is also self-centered and mean. Always was, but he is my son. I loved him and when I told him about Aliel, I wanted him to know he was special. God needed a pure soul, and that's why you were chosen. I also knew no one would believe me. Aliel prepared me for that. With Derwood, I had a good life, but Aliel was, is my true love. He told me all about you and what you would become. You have the power to call other angels. It activated your power when you met Lucifer?"

"Yes ma'am. How did you know that?"

"Aliel told me when your father was two years old. Your power is like a frequency. You will sense demons, any demonic presence, and angels too. Kenya, my dear, you have the same ability. Just know that if you call demons for assistance, it is a direct line to Lucifer. He will know. He has minions everywhere! Darrin is also a catalyst for you. Your power mixed with his strengthens you together, but I feel you already know some of this."

"Yes ma'am, we uh, noticed a power boost recently." Darrin smiled and winked at Kenya who blushed.

"I bet you have, sweetie." Irma winked.

"So is Aliel still around?"

"He still visits from time to time and when the time is right, you will meet him. Until then, you will have your power when you need it and you can command angels. Not all mind you, just those with the same frequency as you and Aliel."

"How do we defeat Lucifer?" Darrin asked.

"The million dollar question! You will fight many battles with Lucifer and more often than not, you will win. But you will not determine his ultimate demise and he, just like you, has his own role to play out on this earth. So stay on your guard, stand your ground, *stick together,* and celebrate your victories. Do not let anyone separate you! The angels in your frequency can help you learn your powers and I will help you any way I can."

"Yes ma'am, will do. Thank you kindly, Grandma Grace."

"You're welcome sweetie. Now, you too have some children to find, yes?" Irma beamed.

"Yes, we do. Thank you so much and I hope to see you again sometime." Kenya said.

"You will my dear, you will. Now come give me another hug," Irma stood and hugged them both. She gave them a lot to process, especially Darrin, but Kenya became more determined than ever to keep him at her side.

Kenya's ringtone, Mr. Grinch for the holiday season, interrupted them and Kenya quickly answered, seeing it was Reina.

"Hey Reina, did you and dad get Danae and her family to the cabin?"

"Yes, but that is not why I am calling you. Mam'zelle's been arrested! She wasted her one phone call on me, but I can't help." Reina said.

"What? Why was she arrested?"

"Not really sure, she said something about losing her immunity and the state is pressing charges for summoning me when I was a demon, to kill for Raymond Bartlett. Can you help her?"

"Damn! That's an automatic death sentence under the Witchcraft Malfeasance Act if they convict her! She needs a good lawyer and even then, our office made the deal. Maybe there is some loophole that the director can use to help. I'll call Dan. Which station is she in?"

"Glenrose Heights and Kenya, she sounded scared." Reina added.

"She has reason to be, but don't worry, I'm on it. You just stay with Daddy. When are you guys coming back?"

"Monday. Your daddy wants to show me around and get some stuff the Gawains may need while they stay here. "

"Okay, I'll keep you posted and see ya when you get back. Love you and give my love to Daddy."

"I will, be careful Kenya and give my love to Darrin."

"I will, thanks." Kenya said before hanging up.

Nine

After making a few phone calls and getting nowhere fast with a defense for Mam'zelle Roca, Kenya had an idea. She quickly pulled up the number for Lucious' law firm in Midtown Atlanta and dialed.

"Well, hello Agent Kenya," Lucious answered.

"Don't you have a secretary to answer your calls?" Kenya said, annoyed that he answered.

"Why bother with a secretary when I knew it was you calling? Besides, you were calling *me*, right?" he replied.

"Yes, I suppose I am. I... I need your help." Kenya

said reluctantly.

"Well, I'll be *damned*! Color me curious. I thought you wanted nothing to do with *me*."

"Well, I... I said that, yes. Under normal circumstances, I would not ask, but..."

"Out with it! I'm getting bored. What do you want me to do?" Lucious said abruptly. He wanted so desperately for her to come to him, any opening would do, but patience was not his strong suit.

"Mam'zelle Roca has been arrested. It's your fault, you know, getting Raymond Bartlett off the way you did. This is a chance to right a wrong."

"And why would I want to do that?"

"Because *I* need her, *Maman Brida* is out of town. I would consider it a personal favor between family." Kenya almost gagged on the word *family*.

"I see, so I convince the state to drop the charges and this will endear me to you?"

"Yes."

"Anything else?"

"Since you asked, yes. Do you know where they are

keeping the children with powers? Powers that *you* gave them, no less. Besides, they are no good to you being locked up and studied like lab rats."

"And what do I get in return?"

"My gratitude."

"And?"

"Well, what do you want?" She said, afraid of the answer, but she saw no other recourse.

"I want to be near my family... I have so many children here and I quite like Atlanta. Like you said, what good are my children to me locked up? I'll give you the location, but *you* will have to rescue them. You are their big sister, blood ties and all. I'll go get Mam'zelle, but now you owe me... dinner at 7pm sharp on Thursdays."

"Every Thursday?"

"Every Thursday."

"Just dinner?"

"Just dinner. You can pick the place. I just want to get to know you."

Kenya thought for a moment. *I think I can live with that knowing the children would be safe, but what if it's a trick? Can I really afford to trust Lucious?*

"Tick Tock, Kenya. What is Mam'zelle's life worth to you and all those poor children?"

"I want her freed today and I want to get those children back home to their parents in time for Christmas."

"Yes, of course."

"Ok, it's a deal." Kenya sighed. *I hope I don't regret this.*

"Done. They have taken the kids to what they have made to look like an industrial warehouse under construction. I have my little minions monitoring the place. Atlanta Industrial off I-285, near Chamblee Dunwoody Road. It's cloaked so you will have to use your power to see it. It's quite the latest technology."

"Great, thank you Lucious."

"You're welcome my dear Kenya." He hung up the phone and smiled to himself. Confident in the deal he made, he buzzed his secretary.

"Yes?" she said through the intercom.

"Sabrina darling, get me Judge Conyers on the phone."

"Right away sir, Mr. Morningside." Sabrina replied.

Kenya set her Samsung phone on the desk. She looked up at Darrin who shook his head, arms folded leaning against the desk beside her.

"I can't believe you literally made a deal with the *devil*! And for a date, no less!" Darrin fumed.

"First off, ew! Second, it's not a date, I'm his great-great descendant or whatever. Besides, I am just using him. It gets Mam'zelle out of jail and the kids free."

"You gonna hide the kids in the mountains too? They're exposed now. How long you think it will take before the government steps in to regulate them like the witches?"

"Maybe we can bind or strip their powers then. It will keep them safe, for now. People have had abilities for years that the government doesn't know about. Let's live to fight another day. You heard your grandma. I say this is a win."

"If we get the kids back, sure. I'll just have to go with you on these 'Thursday night dinners' then. You know, in case, you need backup." Darrin grinned.

"And that's why I love you." Kenya whispered.

"Woman, you outta be glad I love you too!" Darrin

teased.   He leaned in and kissed her lightly on the lips.

"Get a room Selinsky!" An agent yelled from across the room. Darrin shot him the finger and kissed Kenya again.

Ten

Lucious

Raymond's cell rang jarring him from an afternoon nap.

"Hello?" he said sleepily.

"Raymond, your debt is due now." Lucious said.

"What? It's only been little more than a week! I need more time!" Raymond pleaded.

"Your deal says payment will be due anytime *I* deem necessary. I struck a better deal, and I deem it so *now*."

"Wait! Please, who will run my company? I have no heir, no grandchildren!"

"Not a problem, it goes to me." Lucious said as the

fingers of his left hand curled into a fist, his eyes turning black as night.

"But I..." Raymond began to say before he clutched at the pain in his chest, dropping his cell and falling to the ground.

"Debt paid. It was a pleasure doing business with you." Lucious said as he opened his left hand. Placing his cell inside his sport coat, he got out of his car and walked into the police station in Glenrose Heights.

Mam'zelle Roca sat fuming on a cot against the wall in her cell. *This is some bullshit!* She thought to herself. She barely had time to dress before the police dragged her out of bed. Good thing she was wearing one of her many African caftans. She started to shift her body to get comfortable when Lucious appeared outside her cell.

"Oh, HELL no! You get away from me!" she yelled.

"Now is that anyway to talk to *your* attorney?"

"I don't have one and it would never be you!"

"Are you sure about that? I've just come to tell you that you are free to go. *I* got the charges dropped, but if you want to stay..."

"Wait...what? For real?"

"Yes, unless you don't want to go home?"

"I didn't say that naw! So, what you want in return?"

"Nothing, its all taken care of. Need a ride home?"

"Wait, how?"

He opened the cell. "Are we really going to stand here and play twenty questions or do you want a ride home?"

"No, but if it's true, where is the guard?"

"Again with the questions. I don't have all day. Move your ass now!" His eyes flashed black then back to blue, his voice deepened.

Mam'zelle's eyes widened and she jumped up and walked out of the cell. Lucious shut it behind her with a slam and she jumped again.

"If people would just listen the first time, I wouldn't have to be mean. Maybe humans really are daft. I will tell you the 'how and why,' but first you must call Kenya and let her know you are safe. It's number one on speed dial." he smiled as he handed her his phone.

Mam'zelle's hands shook as she took the phone and pressed one. After a few rings, Kenya answered.

"Clark here."

"Kenya, it's me, Mam'zelle Roca. I... I'm out of jail. I'm using Lucious' phone.

"Ok great! Can you meet me at the midtown GBI office? I need your help."

"She wants to know if I can meet her at the midtown GBI place."

"I will have you there within the hour." he said.

"I guess so, I'll be there in about an hour."

"Ok, see ya then." Kenya hung up.

Mam'zelle Roca handed Lucious his phone back.

"See, everything is fine. Now, let's get going, shall we?" he said as he opened the front door of the police station. "Oh, here are your personal affects." He handed her a manila envelope.
"Raymond Bartlett suffered a heart attack and his company and property belong to me now. I'm offering it to you if you are interested. You can use the lab to make your potions into pharmaceutical medicine.

She took the manila envelope and muttered, "Thank you. I'll think about it."
"Well, what have you got to think about? You would be a wealthy woman, no more struggling to keep that pitiful

shop of yours going."

"It sounds too good to be true."

"Do you want it or not?"

"Sure, okay."

"Good, I'll draw up the papers and have you sign next week. Here are the keys to his house. I'm sure you know where it is." Lucious hands her the keys and opens the passenger side door of his black BMW.

Kenya, what have you done?

Eleven

Kenya sat back in her chair. Few agents came to the office on a Saturday, but Kenya got Daniel to come in after she told him where the children were being held.

"What do you mean we can't go get them?" Kenya asked.

"I called the director of the GBI, the FBI, NSA and the CIA and nobody is talking, much less willing to allow us to even enter that building! My hands are tied Kenya."

"God knows what they are doing to those babies and

we don't have clearance? There aren't that many paranormal law enforcement officers and this is definitely paranormal!"

"I don't disagree, but it's a no go and now, they know we know and they may decide to move them to another location. If you go, it's off the books and you'll be risking your career on this one."

"I know Dan, but I have to go. I can't let anymore children or their parents for that matter, suffer or worse, die because I did nothing."

"You saved your friend and her family, isn't that enough?"

"No, I owe it to Mia and Nia, and every child that was given powers that were not their own."

"Ah hell, Selinsky, talk some sense into her!" Daniel pleaded to Darrin.

"You know her better than I do sir, you know she will go with or without your consent." Darrin smiled and shrugged.

"I suppose you are going with her."

"Damn straight, sir."

"Good, who else you got?"

Lucious entered the room with Mam'zelle in tow.

What the devil? "What in the hell is *he* doing here?" Daniel said as he narrowed his eyes at Lucious.

"Backup sir, I need some help, Mam'zelle Roca is going with us." Kenya explained.

"Is the 'prince of darkness' going too?"

"Oh no, I have demons for that. I am just making sure Mam'zelle Roca made it here. My shadow demons are waiting on site, they'll show themselves to you and assist with whatever you need." Lucious said with a grin. His eyes fixed on Kenya. Darrin didn't like it. His eyes began to glow.

"Down boy, tonight we are on the same team." Lucious sneered.

"I doubt that Lucifer, you created this mess in the first doggone place!"

"Well, a fellow needs a little fun now and then. I was only blowing off steam. Still, they are of my bloodline and Kenya has promised to save them, as per our deal."

"You made a deal with Lucifer?" Daniel asked Kenya.

"Yes, it was the only way I could find out where the kids were and free Mam'zelle." Kenya replied. She swallowed hard at Daniel's disappointed look. She wanted to crawl away at that moment, ashamed at asking the devil for help. She stiffened and strengthened her resolve. She would not back down, those children are worth the 'deal' she made.

"Every government agency I mentioned may be waiting for you. It's a fool's errand, a suicide mission!" Daniel tried reasoning with her. Trying to convince her once she made up her mind was useless, but it was one of the many things he admired about her.

"I'll leave you to it then," Lucious said as he left the building.

Kenya called the Hernandez Family. Since they were a family of witches and they had untraceable vans for reasons unknown, not to mention Kenya and Darrin saved their children a few days ago. Angel and Ava agreed along with four gifted cousins.

Next, she contacted the families of the children and coordinated with a few agents to set up safe houses for them. Daniel offered to help, but she wanted him to have plausible deniability in case things went south. He didn't know the details, but knew they were going.

The Hernandez Family, Darrin, Kenya and Mam'zelle

Roca all agreed to meet in two hours. Everyone involved could face jail time and not just any jail, Leavenworth, or worse, they could die. Saving the children is all that mattered to them. Kenya said a quick prayer. What they needed was a miracle.

Twelve

Atlanta Industrial

Kenya and Darrin dressed in black from head to toe along with tactical gear. Both wore black TRU-SPEC BDU pants, which they tucked into their black boots and long sleeve black tees under uniform black polo shirts. Topped off with bullet-proof vests, gloves and a face mask that covered everything but their eyes. They were counting on soldiers and other law enforcement being on site and who would wear the same type of gear.

Killing a fellow agent, officer, or soldier was not part of the plan, only stunning, using gas to put them to sleep and avoidance. It was a line Kenya nor Darrin were willing to cross as Kenya explained to the team once they met up at the south entrance of the construction site.

Kenya focused using her power and she began to see the building inside. Touching the gate surrounding the building, she found her hand passed through it! Everyone stared in amazement.

Angel and Eva Hernandez were on time with two eighteen passenger vans and their four cousins. They were a bit unnerved by the shadow demons they saw hovering near Kenya. Rafael was the only one who could not see them, but he just felt a chill down his spine. None of the Hernandez family had ever met a demon before. It didn't, however, deter them from the task at hand.

Since the shadow demons could go through walls, Kenya instructed them to scout and see how many guards and their location inside and outside the building where the kids were being held.

Eva Hernandez brought her cousins Chuy, Fernanda, and Rubio Ruiz. Angel brought his cousin, Rafael Ramos. They would be the drivers of the two vans that would transport the children to their parents in Forsyth.

Rubio, the eldest brother of Fernanda and Chuy, is

former special ops and acts as a chameleon. He can become whatever surface he touches. His hair style is a buzz cut he maintained after the military.

Fernanda's gift was talking to machines, any machine. She was to disable the digital security, computers, cell phones and radios. Her hair was short, shaved on the left and longer on top covering her right eye. She was short like her cousin Eva, but she was leaner with a tiny waist and sculpted arms.

Chuy, the youngest of the three siblings, can open portals to get from one place to another, which was tricky at times, especially if he didn't know the layout.

Once the shadow demons returned with the intel on the layout, how many guards and where, they agreed to take out as many armed guards as they could without being seen, promising not to kill. Not that Kenya trusted them to keep their promise, but she was grateful for their help.

"There are six younger children in the north side of the building and six older kids are in the east, in glass cages with electronic locks." Tegaan, the head shadow demon told Kenya.

"Okay, remember, no *killing*. Chuy, do you think you can teleport or whatever, and get the older kids out? "

"Not a problem boss lady, but do you trust these demons?" he asked raising an eyebrow.

"We are ordered by our master to give whatever assistance Kenya may require or die." Tegaan said matter-of-factly.

"Damn, that's harsh dude," Chuy said.

"Okay, then… good to know. Darrin, Mam'zelle, and I will go after the younger ones. Eva, Fernanda and Rubio can help with guards. Angel and Rafael, be ready to drive. Meet back here as soon as possible. If you run into trouble, use your coms, and one of us will come. Put on your night vision googles, you'll need them when Fernanda takes out the lights. Fernanda, just take out their coms, not ours, alright?

"I got this Agent Clark, *no problema.* I'll take out the backup generator too." she smiled.

"Good thinking, alright people, move out!" Kenya said.

Fernanda took out the electric fence, the lights, and all forms of communication of the soldiers inside and outside the building. The shadow demons took out guards left and right around and inside the building.

Darrin, Kenya and Mam'zelle, also dressed in black with tactical gear she borrowed from Kenya, made their way inside moving toward the younger children's rooms.

Several doctors and lab techs were running about with flashlights and Kenya threw a flash grenade that blinded them and they dropped the flashlights. Kenya, Darrin and Mam'zelle made their way in the dark past them to the sounds of children crying out in fear.

The first set of rooms Darrin went in had two children, ages 5 and 6. A boy named Carter and his sister Ella.

"Don't be afraid, I'm here to get you out and take you to your parents." Darrin assured them.

Ella, the five-year-old, wrapped her arms around Darrin's leg while her brother, Carter took a little more convincing.

His eyes glowed and it temporarily blinded Darrin who was wearing night vision googles. Darrin felt his own power rise and moving his googles up, showed Carter his glowing green eyes. It was just what Carter needed. To him, Darrin looked liked an angel and he got up and ran to Darrin, gripping his other leg.

"Okay now, it's gonna be tough to walk outta here with ya'll on my legs, so let's say one of you gets on my back and I'll carry the other one in front, alright?"

"Ok, mister," Ella said and reached up.

Darrin picked her up and squatted down so Carter could get on his back. He pressed the com button on his watch. "I've got two, heading back to the south entrance Clark."

"Copy that, I'm getting the twin girls, meet you in the hallway. Any luck Mam'zelle?"

"Yeah, gonna need help with my two, they keep disappearing and these lil suckers are fast too."

"Come again? Disappearing?" Kenya asked.

"Yeah, they keep popping up in different spots and they can see just fine in the dark!"

"I'm in the east wing, what room are you in?" Fernanda asked.

"Room 1008," Mam'zelle replied.

"Copy that, heading your way now. Agent Clark, you and Agent Selinsky get your *ninos* to the van, I've got Mam'zelle."

"*Gracias* Fernanda," Kenya answered.

"Copy that," Darrin said.

"*De nada*." Fernanda replied.

Kenya opened the door and saw Mia and Tia in a room with a two-way mirror. They couldn't see who or what she was and began to scream.

"It's alright girls, it's me, Kenya Clark. We met a few days ago in Empire Park. I tried to help you."

The girls stopped screaming.

"I told you she'd find us!" Kia said.

"We're getting out of here, are you ready?"

"Yes!" the girls replied.

Darrin and Kenya met up in the hallway and made their way back to the south entrance. Mia and Kia held tightly to Kenya's hands as they walked. Shots rang out around the corner and the two agents froze in their tracks. The children were quiet, their hearts pounding.

"Stay here with kids. I'm gonna check it out." Kenya said.

"No, I'll go." Darrin said as he tried to free himself from Carter and Ella, but they held on even tighter, almost choking him.

"Like I said, I'll go." Kenya laughed. Kenya walked ahead, quickly surveying the hallway. It was empty, save a light that emanated from someone standing there motioning her to follow as if guiding her through to a clear path. The light did not blind her with her goggles. She removed her googles to tried make out what she saw. It appeared to be a man, a soft light surrounded him.

She nodded and placing her googles back on, returned to Darrin and the children. Kenya took the girls by the hand and they continued on following what she believed was an angel.

"Did you ask for angelic assistance?" Kenya whispered.

"I wasn't sure it worked. I just thought about it. It just didn't feel right working with demons alone, they could turn on us." Darrin replied. Kenya smiled and nodded, agreeing with his thinking. It is always better to err on the side of caution.

"Agent Clark, this is Chuy, they shot Rubió! He took a bullet to the shoulder. He took on the shape of the wall, but something made him sneeze and they shot him, over."

"Can you get him to the van?" Kenya asked nervously.

"Negative, he's... he's stuck in the wall, boss lady."

"What's your location? This is Eva, over."

"Southeast corridor."

"Open a portal to the van. I'll come to you. I can free him from the wall."

"You got it, Eva."

"Chuy, are the older kids in the van?"

"Yes, just got the last one there. Are you close? Do you need me?" Chuy asked.

"Negative, we've got help and we'll be there soon." Kenya said.

By the time Darrin and Kenya caught up to Chuy and Rubio, the angel disappeared and Eva was moving the wall to release Rubio. Darrin and Kenya continued on their way to the south entrance. They saw the bodies of doctors, soldiers, and lab techs scattered across the floor, some in pieces, and near the doors. *Dammit!*

"Who killed these people? I specifically said, no killing!" Kenya asked angrily over the coms.

"It was one of the older kids, he... uh, retaliated for the way they treated him." Angel replied.

"Okay," Kenya sighed. It had not occurred to her that something like this could happen, but there is no telling what they put these kids through. She really couldn't blame the boy.

"Eva, can do the binding spell now?"

"Already done, Kenya!"

"Copy that, *gracias* Eva."

"*De nada.*"

Kenya reached the other van where Rafael sat waiting with Mam'zelle, a set of twin boys, name Reggie and Raymond, and Fernanda.

"How did you get here before we did?" Kenya asked.

Fernanda and Mam'zelle pointed to Reggie and Raymond who giggled.

"Nice job, boys," Darrin said with wink as he buckled Carter and Ella in the middle seat.

"Thanks," they said in unison.

"Ah Mia, Kia, you two are coming with me and Darrin."

"We are?" they said at the same time.

"Yes, since you don't have foster parents anymore, I

thought maybe you could stay with me and be my little girls?"

"Yes!" they said and hugged Kenya. Kenya hugged them back as a tear slid down her face. She would file papers to adopt them as soon as she could. Her decision to adopt the twins felt right. She felt she could protect them in a way no non-magical person could. She could teach them to harness and handle their powers, regardless how they got them.

"Agent Clark, this is Angel, we are full and good to go. I'm dropping off Rubio with Memia Sanchez then heading to Forsyth."

"Copy that Angel, *gracias*!"

"*De nada Senorita* Clark!"

"We should get going too," Rafael said.

"Yes, by all means, thank you so much!"

"Don't mention it, ever. We were never here." Rafael teased. Everyone laughed. It was late, but their mission was a success.

"Okay, got it. Mam'zelle?"

"On it Kenya, you want me to bind Mia and Kia's powers, too?"

"No, that won't be necessary, will it girls?"

"No ma'am, we'll be good, we promise!"

"Alright, see ya when I get back. Tell Reina to take care of the shop."

"I will. Thank you for your help."

"Anytime and thank you for saving my life!"

"Anytime Mam'zelle, anytime."

Epilogue

Christmas Day

Everyone gathered at Theo's cabin in the mountains to celebrate Christmas. Snow covered the ground and trees. Mia and Kia, along with Jace and Justin, had a snowball fight. Jace has been practicing and was now very good at moving things without his hands. However, Kia used the air to move the snowballs she and Mia made while Mia would zap them with a little heat so that they melted right when they hit their target, Justin. Until he began to stop them in mid-flight.

"No fair," the girls whined. Justin and Jace would just laugh and eventually the girls would too.

Theo decorated the cabin with kente cloth bows and homemade wreaths for the holiday along with a kinara to celebrate Kwanzaa over the next seven days. Homemade gifts for the children surrounded the kinara on the table near the living room.

Theo, Darrin, Carl, and Daniel chopped down the Christmas tree that stood next to the fireplace. The tree was decorated with strings of popcorn, red and gold bulbs, twinkling lights and a sparkling star that Danae made.

Danae and Reina did all the cooking while Kenya and Mam'zelle did all the shopping. Mam'zelle even made her 'special' eggnog. Darrin's parents drove up along with his grandma Grace to join the Clark and Gawain family for Christmas dinner.

After dinner, when everyone was sitting around the fire, Grandma Grace spoke, "Ah Darrin sweetie, didn't you have another gift for Kenya?"

"Ah, yeah, I do, thanks." Darrin walked over to where Kenya was sitting at the dining room table, dug out a box from his right hip pocket and bent on one knee. They heard gasps and sighs all around the room.

"Kenya Denise Clark, will you marry me?" Darrin asked as he opened the velvet box revealing a three-carat diamond solitaire ring.

Kenya's eyes filled with tears. "Yes."

Darrin slid the ring on her finger and kissed her sweetly then hugged her.

Claps, laughter and cheers filled the room. Mia and Kia ran over to the happy couple.

"Does this mean you're gonna be our dad now?" they asked sweetly.

"Why yes, it does little ladies, if that's alright with you?" Darrin knelt down to them. The girls nodded and hugged Darrin tight.

"My great granddaughters! Come, give your Nana Grace a hug!" Irma said as she winked at Kenya and Darrin. The girls rushed to her and gave her a double squeeze.

Theo hugged and congratulated Darrin and Kenya. He looked at Daniel, who stood off to the side looking deep in thought. Theo knew Daniel loved his daughter as well, but he was glad she chose Darrin.

Daniel liked Darrin and could see he and Kenya loved each other and he was happy for them, but part of him felt a twinge of loss and regret.

As for Lucious Morningside, he established his law firm and gained several businesses. He had almost everything he wanted, except Kenya. As he watched the celebration at the cabin on his computer screen, his eyes turned black. They may have won this little battle, but the war was just beginning. He would bide his time, his little succubus, Lissa, had only just begun her seduction of Darrin. Not to mention, he was planning his own seduction of Kenya. Thursday night could not come fast enough.

******

Thank you for reading
The Rise of Lucious Morningside
You can find more books by Mahogany SilverRain at
https://www.mahoganysilverrain.net
This is book two of the Kenya Clark GBI Series, the battle
continues in Book Three.

Other books by Mahogany SilverRain:

*The Grand Dame of Bourbon Street, A Dominique LeRoy
Novel*
Love Bytes A Vampire's Tale
Tell Me You Love Me, Kenya Clark Series Book One
Passion's Pride: Leonessa Book One
Shanghai Sheena
Riona's Luck
A Slave's Heart
Winter's Kiss
Imani's Gift
Sake and Pumpkin Pie
Ebony Encounters: A Trilogy of Erotic Tales

www.ingramcontent.com/pod-product-compliance
Lightning Source LLC
Chambersburg PA
CBHW070508130626
46555CB00003B/1210

* 9 7 8 1 6 4 7 1 3 1 8 1 4 *